Belinda Begins Ballet

by Amy Young

viking

Dedicated to the students at The Village School, who helped brainstorm
this story, to Nancy Baum and her dancing family, and to Maya,
who is an inspiration all on her own.

VIKING

Published by Penguin Group

Penguin Young Readers Group, 345 Hudson Street, New York, New York 10014, U.S.A.

Penguin Books Ltd, Registered Offices: 80 Strand, London WC2R 0RL, England

First published in 2008 by Viking, a division of Penguin Young Readers Group

1 3 5 7 9 10 8 6 4 2

Copyright © Amy Young, 2008

LIBRARY OF CONGRESS CATALOGING-IN-PUBLICATION DATA

Young, Amy.

Belinda begins ballet / by Amy L. Young.

p. cm.

Summary: When Belinda, a tiny girl with enormous feet, is cast as a clown in her school's talent show
she is very unhappy, but after each disastrous rehearsal she observes an older student ballet dancing,
then goes home to practice what she has seen.

ISBN 978-0-670-06244-7 (hardcover)

[1. Foot—Fiction. 2. Talent shows—Fiction. 3. Ballet dancing—Fiction. 4. Size—Fiction.] I. Title.

PZ7.Y845Bdv 2008

[E]—dc22   2007021675

Manufactured in China
Set in Mrs. Eaves Roman and Weehah

Once there was a beautiful baby named Belinda. Everything about Belinda was tiny—well, almost everything . . .

She had a tiny curl on her head,

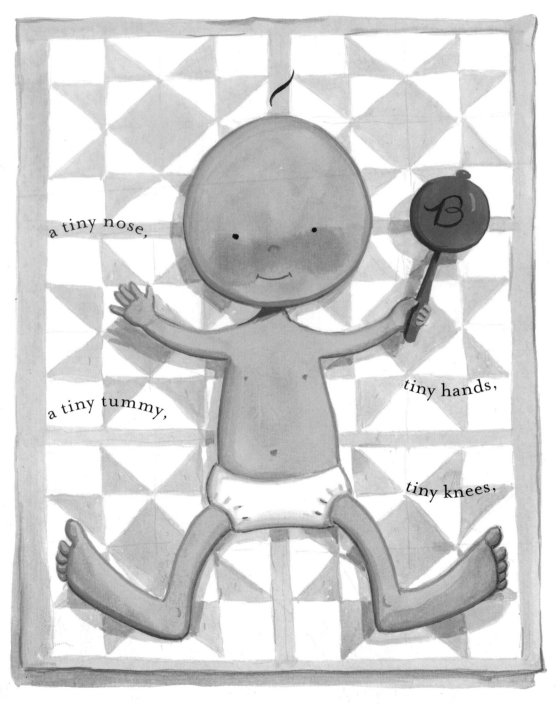

a tiny nose,

tiny hands,

a tiny tummy,

tiny knees,

and—MY GOODNESS!
Great big enormous feet!

"Oh, well," people said. "She'll grow into them."

She did not grow into them.
Instead, Belinda's feet just kept
getting bigger.

As Belinda grew older, she realized that big feet could be useful.

She could reach the cookie jar.

She could also jump very high on the trampoline, although she usually landed in a tree.

She was excellent at soccer, but she had more fun leaping across the field and doing victory dances than scoring goals.

She could ski without even
using skis, although her toes got cold.

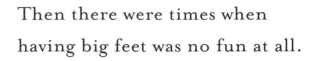 Then there were times when
having big feet was no fun at all.

Jumping rope was hard,

and so was playing hopscotch.

Shopping for shoes was a nightmare. The shoes
that fit were usually really ugly.

But the worst was the day Mrs. Rhino, the drama teacher, picked Belinda to be a clown in the school talent show. Belinda had gone to watch her friends JJ and Kirsten try out their juggling routine. Mrs. Rhino signed them up. Then her eye fell on Belinda. "What's your talent?" she demanded.

"I don't have a talent," said Belinda.

"Well, with those big feet, you'd be a great clown! We need a clown. You'll go on before your friends."

"But I don't want—" said Belinda.

"No buts," said Mrs. Rhino.

Rehearsals started the next day after school.

"Ready, Belinda?" said Mrs. Rhino. "Spin on your heels, then fall on your bottom.

"Next, spin on your toes, and fall on your face."

Belinda had no choice. She had to learn the clown dance. "Fall harder! That's it!" shouted Mrs. Rhino. "With those feet, you're a natural!"

Belinda was mortified.

At the end of rehearsal, she threw off the clown costume and ran out of the room. Belinda wanted to hide, so she slipped into the dark auditorium.

A light went on, and Belinda realized she was not alone. One of the older students was on the stage, dressed as a ballerina. Miss Tweet, the dance teacher, sat in the front row.

"All right, Camille," said Miss Tweet. "Let's see that piece again. You are almost ready for the talent show."

Beautiful music filled the room. Camille flitted and wove through the air like a butterfly.

Belinda forgot her troubles. She wanted to dance like that.

She hurried home
and practiced dancing
in her room.

She pretended she was a bird.

The next day, rehearsal for the clown dance was even worse.

"Don't be afraid to get dirty!" snorted Mrs. Rhino. "Great job! You and your feet are so funny!"

Belinda didn't feel funny; she felt miserable. After rehearsal she snuck into the auditorium again, where once again Camille was rehearsing. As Belinda watched, she felt lighter and happier.

Belinda tiptoed out and rushed home to practice. She learned to spin gracefully without wavering, and she tried to hold her leg up high above her head.

After every clown rehearsal, Belinda went to watch Camille dance, and then she went home to practice what she saw.

By the time the talent show came around,
Belinda could leap clear over her bed and spin
many times in a row without stopping.

On the night of the talent show, Mrs. Rhino gave
Belinda a pep talk. "Remember, the clumsier you are,
the better. Just let those big feet do their thing!"

A dancer floated gracefully by. It was Camille, on her way to perform. "Haven't I seen you somewhere?" Camille said.

Belinda smiled shyly.

Belinda watched from backstage as Camille leapt and pirouetted. She moved so beautifully! All too soon, the dance ended.

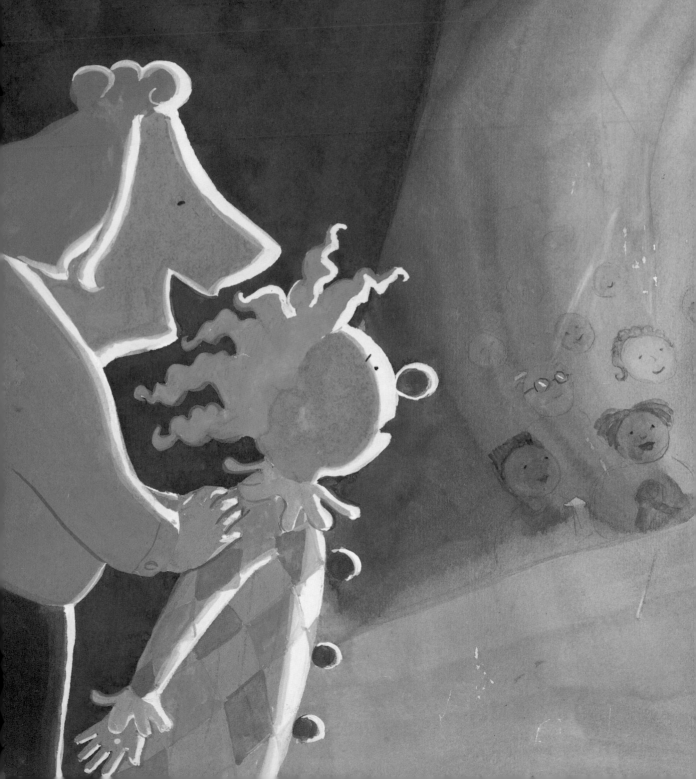

"You're on!" Mrs. Rhino pushed Belinda onto the stage.

The goofy music started, and Belinda began her routine.
She spun on her heels and fell on her behind. The audience
guffawed and hooted.

Then Belinda spun on her toes, but
instead of falling on her face, like a
clown, she remembered how it felt
to dance like a ballerina.

Without even meaning to, she leapt lightly into the air and twirled around, and then kicked out her legs and did a split.

"Ooh," said the audience.

"HEY!" said Mrs. Rhino.

Belinda swirled gracefully across the stage. She ended with six pirouettes in a row, and then curtsied to the audience. Applause and cheers rang in her ears.

When Belinda got backstage, Mrs. Rhino thundered,

"That wasn't funny at all!"

Camille won the talent show. As she passed Belinda
with her trophy, she said, "You're a natural! I hope
you'll keep dancing!"

"Oh, yes—I will!" Belinda smiled.

Belinda did keep dancing. She studied ballet, and won the talent show the very next year.

"Too bad," sighed Mrs. Rhino sadly.

"She could have been such a great clown."